GRANNY'S QUILT

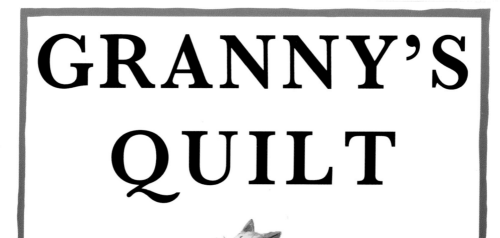

PENNY IVES

Hamish Hamilton • London

I have the best granny in the world. I love going to stay
with her and her two cats Fred and Mr Big, and I always
ask Granny to tell me the story of her wonderful
patchwork quilt. And Granny always says: "Do you really

UWE
BRISTOL
University of the
West of England

UWE BRISTOL
WITHDRAWN
LIBRARY SERVICES

REDLAND
LIBRARY

7000346578

This book should be returned by the last date
stamped below.

09. FEB 1998	1st Dec 99	6
09. FEB 1998	18. JAN 2000	
17 FEB 1998	09. MAY 2000	27. OCT 2003
24. MAR 1998	11. DEC 2000	15. FEB 2005
08. JUL 1998	21. FEB 2001	16. MAR 2005
	07. JUN 2001	13. APR 2005
09. DEC 1998	20 DEC 2001	
23. FEB 1999	30 APR 2002	
27. APR 1999	01. DEC 2004	

BRISTOL UWE   B1084/10/92
Printing & Stationery Services

Y

Patchwork History Families CF

**REDLAND LIBRARY
UNIVERSITY OF THE WEST OF
ENGLAND, BRISTOL
REDLAND HILL
BRISTOL BS6 6UZ**

HAMISH HAMILTON LTD

Published by the Penguin Group
27 Wrights Lane, London W8 5TZ, England
Penguin Books USA Inc, 375 Hudson Street, New York, New York 10014, U.S.A.
Penguin Books Australia Ltd, Ringwood, Victoria, Australia.
Penguin Books Canada Ltd, 10 Alcorn Avenue, Toronto, Ontario, Canada M4V 3B2
Penguin Books (NZ) Ltd, 182-190 Wairau Road, Auckland 10, New Zealand.

Penguin Books Ltd, Registered Offices: Harmondsworth, Middlesex, England.

First Published in Great Britain 1993 by Hamish Hamilton Ltd

Copyright © 1993 by Penny Ives

1 3 5 7 9 10 8 6 4 2

The moral right of the author has been asserted
All rights reserved. Without limiting the rights under copyright reserved above, no part of this
publication may be reproduced, stored in or introduced into a retrieval system or transmitted, in
any form or by any means (electronic, mechanical, photocopying, recording or otherwise), without
the prior written permission of both the copyright owner and the above publisher of this book.

British Library Cataloguing in Publication Data
CIP data for this book is available from the British Library

ISBN 0-241-13274-6

Printed in Italy by L.E.G.O. SpA

want to hear that old nonsense again? I must have told
you about the quilt a thousand times. You know, it's like
the story of my life. The little pieces are from all my
different dresses, ever since I was a small girl just like you."

"I had ten brothers and sisters. My mother, who was a dressmaker, made all our clothes. Mine were usually hand-me-downs, but I had a new dress of my very own for my baby sister Emily's christening. It was made from this lovely blue spotty material."

"'Make do and mend' was my mother's motto. These faded pieces with the pink flowers came from my eldest sister Agnes Ann's best dress.

Then my clever mother cut it up and turned it into bloomers for Violet and an everyday frock for Rose.

Next time round she unpicked all the seams and made summer smocks for Babs and Maggie.

Finally, Mother made Rose a swimsuit – and a sun-dress for me with a matching hat, out of the last bits of the material."

"These squares are from my school pinafore.
I hated the dark blue cloth! I was always being
told off in school for day dreaming.

One day a girl called Margaret Muddle brought in her
pet mouse. Everyone was allowed to see it except for me –
I'd been sent to stand in the corner!"

"This lavender satin was my first dance frock. Oh how I loved it! Mother was making an evening gown for a titled lady, and there was just enough material left over for a dress for me. It was all the rage then to have a boyish figure. I had to flatten my bust by tying a long scarf round and round. I always crossed my fingers that it wouldn't come undone in the middle of a Charleston!"

"When I was a bit older I went out to work as a
children's nanny. It was harder in those days – there
weren't many jobs for girls to choose from. I wore a grey

dress and a white head-square which I thought made me look like a nun. One day in the park, a handsome man came and sat next to me. He asked me out to tea, and then five years later he asked me to marry him! The handsome man was your grandpa!"

"The white silk is from my wedding dress. It had pearl buttons all the way down the back. I saved my wages for months to buy the material. I remember that it was such a windy day my veil kept blowing over my eyes!"

"This piece of material with little boats sailing all over it is from a dress with a dancing sailor on the pocket. I wore it when *your* mummy was a baby and Grandpa and I used to go down to the beach with our tea. I had that dress until it almost fell apart."

"The squares of blue and green leaves
bring back such memories. They're cut
from a war-time dress. I wore it the day
your mummy and I were evacuated to the
country. We had to save up our clothing
coupons for ages to buy anything new, so
that dress had to last the whole war.
I remember how we all had to take
our gas masks with us.
Your mummy *hated* hers!"

"I made this yellow material covered in little black bees into a pinafore. I wore it every day for housework and I thought it seemed just right – busy bees just like me. Sometimes your mummy helped me when she came home from school – but sometimes she didn't!"

"Let's put the quilt back on the bed, now," said Granny. "That's the end of the patchwork quilt story. The busy bee pinafore dress was the last one I saved. We'll have to look at my photo album to see what happened next.

That's your mummy's wedding photo. I wore my best hat with the yellow silk ribbon that day.

And this one was taken at your christening.

And here's one that was taken only two years ago. I made you that little dress, do you remember? I even have some of the material left! Perhaps *you* could start a patchwork quilt?"

And today Granny showed me how to make a patchwork quilt of my own. Now when I grow up *my* quilt will tell a story just like hers.